HEIDI HECKELBECK

Lends a Helping Hand

By Wanda Coven

Illustrated by Priscilla Burris

LITTLE SIMON

New York London Toronto Sydney New Delhi

LITTLE SIMON
An imprint of Simon & Schuster Children's Publishing Division
1230 Avenue of the Americas, New York, New York 10020
First Little Simon hardcover edition May 2019
Copyright © 2019 by Simon & Schuster, Inc.
Also available in a Little Simon paperback edition.
All rights reserved, including the right of reproduction in whole or in part in any form. LITTLE SIMON is a registered trademark of Simon & Schuster, Inc., and associated colophon is a trademark of Simon & Schuster, Inc. For information about special discounts for bulk purchases, please contact Simon & Schuster Special Sales at 1-866-506-1949 or business@simonandschuster.com. The Simon & Schuster Speakers Bureau can bring authors to your live event. For more information or to book an event contact the Simon & Schuster Speakers Bureau at 1-866-248-3049 or visit our website at www.simonspeakers.com.
Designed by Ciara Gay
Manufactured in the United States of America 0419 FFG
10 9 8 7 6 5 4 3 2 1
Library of Congress Cataloging-in-Publication Data
Names: Coven, Wanda, author. | Burris, Priscilla, illustrator.
Title: Heidi Heckelbeck lends a helping hand / by Wanda Coven ; illustrated by Priscilla Burris. | Description: New York : Little Simon, [2019] | Series: Heidi Heckelbeck ; #26 | Summary: Heidi discovers that helping to clean up can be fun, so she brings her community together to make the neglected "Trash Park" beautiful again. | Identifiers: LCCN 2018039077 | ISBN 9781534445291 (pbk) | ISBN 9781534445307 (hc) | ISBN 9781534445314 (eBook)
Subjects: | CYAC: Parks—Fiction. | Community life—Fiction. | Helpfulness—Fiction. | Witches—Fiction.
Classification: LCC PZ7.C83393 Hkg 2019 | DDC [Fic]—dc23
LC record available at https://lccn.loc.gov/2018039077

CONTENTS

Chapter 1

SLiME TiME!

Splurt!

Splurt!

Splurt!

Heidi Heckelbeck squeezed a glob of craft glue into a mixing bowl. Then she squirted some shaving cream on top.

Next she sprinkled some contact lens solution into the mix. Finally, she added the special liquid activator.

Heidi swirled the ingredients together like a magic potion—only this wasn't actually a potion.

Today, in her art class, she was making a huge bowl of *slime*. Fluffy slime, to be exact.

She stirred until the slime pulled away from the bowl and became a big fluff-o-luscious *blob*. Then she pulled the slime with all ten fingers.

"It's so squishable!" she said, squeezing it with her hands.

Lucy Lancaster, who was sitting next to Heidi, peeked into Heidi's bowl.

"Oooh!" she exclaimed, stirring her own mix faster to catch up. "Your slime looks so marshmallowy!"

Heidi grabbed her slime and kneaded it like bread dough. The slime spoke a language all its own: *Skloop! Sklorp! Skleep!*

"Time to add some color!" Heidi announced. She plopped the slime back in the bowl and opened a package of neon-green powdered food coloring.

She dumped the whole package of dye into the bowl. Then she slapped the slime with her hand. *POOF!* The powder burst into a neon-green cloud and speckled Heidi's face.

The palm of her hand turned bright green too.

She squished and squashed the dye into the mix until it all blended.

"And now for some slime mix-ins!" Heidi grabbed a fistful of Styrofoam beads and then smooshed them into her slime to make slime-a-floam. *Squish! Squash! Snap! Crackle!*

Melanie Maplethorpe, who was
sitting across from Heidi, poured a
whole tube of pink-silver sparkles
into her slime and mashed them in.
Then she held up her hot-pink slime
for everyone to see.

"MY slime is the pinkest slime in the WHOLE world!" Melanie declared. "And the sparkliest!"

By the end of the class, the art room was a gloopy, gloppy, capital *M* Mess. Puddles of glue and shaving

cream dotted the tables. The chairs
and the tabletops had splotches of
green, pink, purple, and yellow dye.
Glitter twinkled on top of everything
like fairy dust.

"Cleanup time!" Mr. Doodlebee called. He handed out plastic containers to store the slime. But everybody kept right on squishing and squashing.

Mr. Doodlebee had to whistle through his fingers to get the students' attention. "*Please* put your slime away and clean up your areas! It's time for lunch."

Now the children hopped to it. They stored their slime and washed their hands.

Mr. Doodlebee looked at his watch. The desks were still a mess and the bell was going to ring in three, two, one . . .

Ring!

Mr. Doodlebee laughed and waved the kids out. "Saved by the bell. I'll finish cleaning, class."

The students filed out of the room. Heidi noticed Mr. Doodlebee cleaning up some of the Styrofoam beads she had spilled. She stopped for a moment. *I really want to help him clean up,* she thought.

Then Lucy called out, "Hurry up, Heidi! I'm hungry."

Heidi turned to her friend, then looked back at her teacher.

Mr. Doodlebee DID say he'd finish the cleaning, she thought.

"Wait up, Lucy!" Heidi called as she grabbed her lunch box. "All that squishing made me hungry too!"

SODA SPLAT

Back at home Heidi and her little brother, Henry, checked the kitchen counter for the popcorn popper. Mom always left the popper out on Fridays—that's because Friday was Movie Night at the Heckelbecks'. And Movie Night meant popcorn!

But instead of the popcorn popper, the kids found two pairs of safety goggles and two white lab coats lying on the counter.

"Why are these here?" Henry asked.

Heidi shrugged. "I dunno, but I sure could have used one of these lab coats in art today," she said. "Because we made slime."

Henry's face lit up. "SLIME?! Wow, you're SO lucky! All we got to do today was work in the school garden. BOR-ing!"

Heidi laughed. "The school garden isn't THAT bad," she said. "I like digging in the dirt."

Henry scrunched up his face. "Not me."

Then the door creaked open and
Mom and Dad walked in from Dad's
lab.

"Hey, kiddos! Time to put on your
lab coats and goggles!" Dad said.

Heidi and Henry looked at each
other.

"Wait. But what about Movie Night?"
Heidi asked.

Dad patted Heidi on the shoulder.
"We are going to mix things up
tonight," he said, rubbing his hands
together enthusiastically. "Because

this Friday night, the Heckelbecks are going to invent a new *healthy* soda!"

Heidi's father worked for a soda company called The Fizz. He always came up with wild ideas, but this might be his wildest.

The kids stared blankly at him.

"Who ever heard of healthy soda?"
Heidi said uncertainly.

Dad pointed both pointer fingers
at Heidi like she had just won a door
prize.

"Nobody has!" he cheered. "That's
why we're going to be the first ones
to invent it."

"The goal is to use these ingredients to create a delicious, healthy soda," Dad said. "We'll each make two sodas, and then we'll have a sampling session."

Everyone got to work.

In round one, Mom made sweet corn soda. Dad mixed together kale, spinach, and avocado into a very superbright green and sparkling soda.

Henry dreamed up something that he called Dark Chocolate Mulberry Fizz. And Heidi tried blending fresh strawberries with cold vanilla almond milk for a

strawberry-vanilla soda.

In round two, Mom made a bubbly carrot-and-cucumber soda. Dad brewed a fresh ginger–cinnamon–turmeric ale. Henry whipped up peanut butter and jelly soda, while Heidi prepared a watermelon fizz.

"Now to taste our creations!" Dad said. He poured the drinks into paper cups.

Heidi sipped Dad's green soda first and wiped her mouth with the back of her hand. "Blech!" she cried. "This tastes like pond scum cola!"

She chugged some water to get the taste out of her mouth.

Henry glugged down a glass of his peanut butter and jelly soda. *"Mmmmmm!"* he said. "This one tastes like my favorite LUNCH— only with BUBBLES!"

Heidi tried it and liked it too.

After tasting all the sodas, the family wrote down their favorite flavors. Dad counted the votes, and it was a tie.

"And the winners *are* . . ." Dad paused for a moment to build the excitement. Then he did the big reveal. "Strawberry Vanilla Almond Milk soda and PB and J soda!"

Heidi and Henry both pumped their fists triumphantly.

"Congratulations, kids!" Dad cried. "I'll tweak your recipes over the weekend and present them to my group on Monday. But first we have to clean up the lab."

Heidi looked around. It was every bit as bad as Mr. Doodlebee's art room after a slime session.

"Don't worry about the mess," Mom said. "It's getting late, so I'll help Dad clean up. You kids get ready for bed."

As Heidi took off her stained lab coat, she

watched her parents get to work. They were laughing and playing while cleaning! It looked like they were actually having fun! Heidi thought that was pretty cool.

She was about to offer to help when Henry yelled, "Race you upstairs!"

"You're on!" cheered Heidi as she sprinted after him.

Chapter 3

TRASH PARK

Heidi's stomach rumbled. "Wow! I am starving," she told Lucy as they both walked to Bruce Bickerson's house for a Saturday cookout. Heidi could almost smell the hot dogs and hamburgers on the grill.

Then Lucy's stomach rumbled back.

"Me too!" Lucy said. "Let's take the shortcut through Trash Park."

The park near Bruce's house was really called Trace Park, but it had been dumpy for so long that everyone called it "Trash Park."

The girls found the entrance path. It had become a tunnel of twisted, overgrown shrubs.

Heidi swished the twigs and creepers away from her face. "This park is more like a JUNGLE!"

Lucy unhooked her sleeve from a pricker bush. "You're not kidding!" she said.

The girls continued down the cracked walkway and crossed a meadow of weeds. In the middle of the meadow stood some rotted picnic tables and some old tires. Heidi stared at a broken-down teeter-totter and a swing set without any swings sticking up from the weeds.

"It looks haunted," Heidi said.

Lucy nodded as the girls passed some forgotten gardens choked with weeds. Then Heidi and Lucy noticed an elderly couple sitting on a rundown bench in the sunshine. The woman sprinkled bread crumbs onto the ground.

"Look!" Lucy whispered. "That lady is feeding the birds."

Heidi stopped and watched the birds peck at the crumbs. The couple laughed as the birds fluttered around them.

Wow, Heidi thought. *That couple looks so happy—even though they're in the middle of this dingy old park.* A warm, fuzzy feeling washed over her.

Then Lucy tapped Heidi on the shoulder. "Hello? Earth to Heckelbeck!" she said. "This is supposed to be a shortcut. *Remember?*"

Heidi shook her head and snapped out of her daydream. "Oh yeah!" she said. "What are we waiting for?"

Chapter 4

BACK iN THE SLIME-A-TORY

"Slime time!" Heidi exclaimed in art class on Monday. Mr. Doodlebee had let the kids bring their own mix-ins this time.

"Instead of a laboratory, we should call this the SLIME-a-tory!" Bruce said as he lined up his ingredients.

He had brought in toothpaste, baby oil, shower gel, and glow-in-the-dark paint.

Melanie reached into her pink polka-dot shopping bag and pulled out a sack of sparkly purple sand. She mixed some into her fresh, new slime.

"Everyone look at my beautiful slime!" she cried, tilting her bowl and moving it from left to right so everyone could see. "It has shimmering swirls!" Then she bumped her bag of purple sand, and it poured onto the art room floor.

"Oopsies!" Melanie snickered.

Heidi rolled her eyes. *What a mess!* she thought.

Melanie tried to set the bag of sand upright, but it tipped the other way, and the rest of the sand spilled onto the table.

But Melanie was not the only one making a huge mess. Even Bruce squiggled toothpaste all over the table.

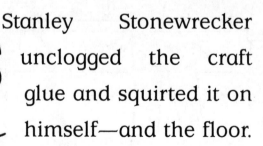

Stanley Stonewrecker unclogged the craft glue and squirted it on himself—and the floor.

Heidi even heard some of her own beads tick onto the floor.

When the bell rang, the art room looked like it had been hit by a craft cloudburst all over again. Globs of different-colored slime stuck to the tables like wads of old bubble gum. Glue dribbles led to paint smears, which were topped with confetti, sand, sparkles, and tiny beads.

Poor Mr. Doodlebee, Heidi thought. *He's stuck with another HUGE mess.*

Then Heidi had an idea. She walked up to Mr. Doodlebee and tapped him on the shoulder.

"May I stay and help you clean up?" she asked.

Mr. Doodlebee let out a big smile. "Why, that would be wonderful, Heidi. What a nice, caring offer! In fact, Mrs. Welli will join us too."

50

Then he handed Heidi a dustpan and brush. "Would you sweep the tabletops off?"

"Sure!" Heidi said.

She held the dustpan at the edge of each table and swept the leftover mix-ins into it. Some of the scraps fell onto the floor, so she tried to be more careful with her next swipe.

When she was done, Heidi gathered all the empty slime bowls and placed them in the sink. She squeezed dish soap on top of them and ran the water. The bubbles began to grow and grow until the foam rose higher than the sink. Heidi batted the bubbles down

with a scrub brush. Then she washed the bowls and stacked them on the dish racks.

With Mrs. Welli and Heidi helping Mr. Doodlebee, the cleanup went fast. Mr. Doodlebee stopped sweeping and admired their work.

"Thanks, Heidi. You really helped
make my classroom look beautiful
again," he said.

Heidi beamed. "It was fun!" she
said.

As she skipped toward the cafeteria
to meet up with her friends and eat
lunch, a new feeling came over Heidi.
Not only was helping fun, it made her
feel good, too!

Chapter 5

SURPRISE DAY

On Wednesday, Aunt Trudy picked Heidi up from school. Every other week Heidi and her aunt would do something fun together—just the two of them. Aunt Trudy did the same thing for Henry. She called it their Surprise Day.

"Would you like to go to the Enchanted Forest?" suggested Aunt Trudy.

The Enchanted Forest was the coolest toy store in town. It had a giant tree house, a play castle, and tons of toys.

"No, thanks. Not today," Heidi said, buckling her seat belt.

Aunt Trudy drove out of the parking lot. "How about Happy Hollow?" she suggested.

Heidi loved Happy Hollow. It had a petting zoo and rides.

"No, thanks," Heidi said again.

Aunt Trudy switched on her blinker and pulled over to the side of the road until they knew where they were going. "Would you like to paint pottery?"

"Not in the mood."

"Go to the library?"

"Nah."

"Zip line?"

"Uh-uh."

"Bowling?"

"Nope."

"Ice cream?"

"Not now."

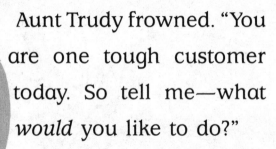

Aunt Trudy frowned. "You are one tough customer today. So tell me—what *would* you like to do?"

Heidi turned toward her aunt. "I'd really like to go to Trash Park."

Aunt Trudy thrust her head back. "Why would you want to go there?" she asked. "It's so ugly and overgrown. We could go to the new park. They have a butterfly exhibit and Frisbee golf."

Heidi shrugged. "Trash Park isn't *that* bad. And besides, I think the park needs us."

Aunt Trudy chuckled. "It needs a lot more than just us."

Now it was Heidi's turn to frown. *"Please?"*

Aunt Trudy took a deep breath. "Well, okay," she agreed. "If that's what you really want to do."

Heidi sat up straight in her seat. "Yup!" she said. "That's what I really want to do!"

Chapter 6

NO MAGIC ANSWER

Aunt Trudy pulled up in front of Trash Park. There were no cars around. "Here we are," she announced. "And it looks like we're the only ones here."

Heidi hopped out of the car and waited on the sidewalk. "COME ON!" she said excitedly.

"Are you *sure* this is an entrance?" Aunt Trudy asked as she looked at the archway of overgrown bushes.

Heidi turned around. "It's like a tunnel," she said. "Isn't it cool?"

Aunt Trudy brushed a swarm of gnats away from her face. "Sooo cool . . . ," she said uncertainly.

They walked to the meadow. Heidi pointed out the swing set with no swings and the broken-down teeter-totter.

Then Heidi saw the same elderly couple she and Lucy had seen the other day.

"Look!" Heidi cried, pointing. "It's THEM!"

Aunt Trudy waved nervously to the couple, who had heard Heidi. They both had on work gloves and straw hats. The woman held a trowel and a watering can. The man carried a flat of white daisies and purple asters. They waved back.

"Do you know them?" Aunt Trudy asked.

"Not exactly," Heidi admitted. "What do you think they're doing?"

Aunt Trudy and Heidi watched as the couple walked along a winding path and stopped in front of a small

row of flowers blooming between a pair of overgrown bushes.

"Look! They have their very own garden!" Heidi gasped. "Right here! In the middle of Trash Park!"

Aunt Trudy and Heidi admired the garden from a distance. The flower bed had been outlined in stones.

"It's so pretty," Aunt Trudy said as they watched the elderly couple plant more flowers. Then she put her arm around Heidi. "Is *this* why you brought me here? Do *you* want to make Trace Park beautiful again?"

Heidi bobbed her head up and down. "Yes!" she cried. "Can you help me, Aunt Trudy? Can we come up with a spell?"

Aunt Trudy squeezed Heidi close to her side. "I'm not sure the *Book of Spells* has a magic answer for a project like this. But maybe I can help you."

Heidi threw her arms around her aunt. "Thank you! I just *knew* you would understand."

Aunt Trudy looked her niece right in the eye. "Make no mistake, it's going to be a *lot* of hard work," she warned.

Heidi flexed her arm muscles. "No problem!" she said. "I LIKE hard work! And do you know what else I like?"

Aunt Trudy raised an eyebrow. "Ice cream?" she guessed.

"Correct-a-mundo!" Heidi cried. "Race you to the car!"

Chapter 7

ACTiON PLAN

Heidi and Aunt Trudy needed to round up a cleanup crew to save Trace Park. First Aunt Trudy got permission from the town of Brewster and notified Brewster's Parks and Recreation Volunteer Program. Then she sent an e-mail asking her friends for help.

At home Heidi designed a special
flyer that said:

SAVE TRACE PARK!

What: Cleanup Day!

When: Saturday, May 5,

8 a.m. until 5 p.m.

Where: Trace Park

Please bring gloves, rakes, shovels,

trowels, brooms, garbage bags, and

snacks to share.

Heidi drew a garland of flowers as a border around her flyer and a little red wheelbarrow in the bottom corner. She showed the flyer to her parents.

"It's beautiful, Heidi," Dad said. "And I would like to donate a large Dumpster to your cleanup day."

Heidi hugged her Dad.

"And I'm going to ask my friends at Rolling Stone Nursery to donate flowers and plants," Mom said.

Heidi clapped her hands. "That would be so perfect!" she cried.

Henry wanted to help too. He stood in front of Heidi with his hands behind his back. "Guess which hand?"

Heidi pointed to Henry's left hand.

"Good guess!" he said, and he pulled a plastic robotic arm out from behind his back.

"I can pick up tons of trash with this," he said. Then he squeezed the trigger at the top of the robotic arm, and the claw opened and closed.

"Cool!" Heidi said.

Henry held out the robotic arm, and Heidi shook its hand—or rather, claw.

The next day Heidi, Lucy, and Bruce made copies of her flyer and handed them out all over school. Principal Pennypacker even made a "Save Trace Park" announcement over the loudspeaker.

Soon everyone began to talk about saving Trace Park. After school Heidi and her friends slipped flyers in the mailboxes in the neighborhood.

"Do you think anyone will show up?" Heidi said.

Lucy placed the last flyer into a white mailbox. "Of course!" she said. "*I* will—for one!"

She held out her hand—palm side down—in front of her friends.

"Me too!" Bruce agreed, laying his hand on top of Lucy's.

"Me three!" Heidi added. Then she placed her hand on top of Bruce's, and they were all in.

Chapter 8

ROLL UP YOUR SLEEVES!

Neighbors and friends from all over Brewster arrived at Trace Park on Saturday morning. They had shovels, clippers, rakes, and lots of other gardening tools and supplies.

Bruce's dad even brought his tractor and began to mow the meadow.

Heidi's mother and Aunt Trudy started clipping overgrown bushes with hedge trimmers. Then Heidi's dad dragged the branches into a pile for composting.

Henry picked up stray trash with his shiny robotic claw. And Heidi and her friends pulled weeds, like thistles, dandelions, and crab grass.

"What a fantastic turnout!" Heidi told Lucy. "Even Melanie showed up!"

Lucy yanked a dandelion up by its roots. "But she's not exactly working. She's just bossing people around."

Heidi watched Melanie shouting orders.

"Pick up that piece of trash!" directed Melanie, pointing out an empty french fry carton to Henry. "And will somebody please move this GIANT rock?"

Heidi grumbled, "What a bossy boss lady!"

Aunt Trudy, who had been listening in, stopped trimming for a moment. "Well, I think it's nice that Melanie came to support *your* cause, Heidi," she said. "It shows she actually cares."

Heidi smiled. *Wow,* she thought. *Melanie is actually supporting MY project.*

Then a red pickup truck rumbled beside the park. It was Principal Pennypacker and Mr. Doodlebee. They unloaded lots of wood and power tools. Then they set up two sawhorses and unfolded some building plans.

"Are they going to make new park benches?" Heidi exclaimed.

Lucy stood up to see. "And new picnic tables!" she cried.

The hum and buzz of hard work echoed through the morning air. Slowly, Heidi began to believe they could actually make Trace Park beautiful again.

Chapter 9

MAKEOVER

Mrs. Richards, the owner of Rolling Stone Nursery, unloaded flowers and plants from the back of her truck. Heidi and Lucy ran to greet her.

"May we help?" Heidi asked.

Mrs. Richards held out a purple flower. "Of course!" she said.

The girls helped carry the plants. Then they cleared a space for the new flower beds. Mrs. Richards helped them scoop holes and place the flowers in the dirt. Then they pushed the loose dirt into the holes and patted it with their fingertips.

Nearby, Bruce and Stanley rubbed wood stain on the new park benches.

Melanie, of course, helped by directing the boys. "You missed a spot!" she shouted. "Don't forget to do the BACK!"

In the middle of the park, some grown-ups had prepared tables with sandwiches, chips, and grapes. Pitchers of ice water and lemonade sat at the end of each table. At noon everyone took a break for lunch.

Heidi popped a grape in her mouth. Then she noticed the elderly couple who had the secret garden. They were walking in her direction. She waved to them.

"Are you the one responsible for this cleanup day?" the woman asked.

Heidi nodded and explained how she had organized the Save Trace Park project.

"This reminds me of what the park used to look like when I was a little girl," the woman said.

Then she pointed to the old tires lying in the meadow. "You see those tires? They used to hang from ropes in the trees. We used them as swings."

This made her husband laugh. "I remember that," he said. "And when the ropes broke, we used the tires for bases in our kickball games."

Everyone gathered around to hear stories of what Trace Park had been like in the past.

"What a wonderful idea to invite the whole community to restore this park," the woman said.

Aunt Trudy put her arm around Heidi. "It was all Heidi's idea," she said. "We just came to lend her a hand."

The man and woman thanked Heidi and said, "Now, how can we help?"

Chapter 10

LiVE ON 5!

By the end of the day Trace Park looked like new.

"Why didn't we do this sooner?" Aunt Trudy asked as she admired their work.

Heidi's mom took off her gardening gloves and ruffled Heidi's hair.

"It's because nobody thought of it until one clever girl had a grand idea," she said.

Heidi blushed pink. "Well, all Trace Park needed was just a helping hand," she said.

"It needed a lot *more* than just a helping hand," Henry said as he tugged Heidi's arm with his robotic claw.

Heidi brushed the claw away and corrected herself. "Okay, it needed a lot of helping hands . . . and one robotic arm."

Henry clacked his robotic pinchers happily.

Then an unexpected van pulled up alongside the park. It had a satellite dish on top. On the side of the van in fancy lettering was the slogan: LIVE ON 5.

"Is that the local TV station?" asked Bruce. "What are they doing here?"

A lady in a gray suit and a thin red scarf stepped out of the van. She had a stylish pixie haircut and silver earrings, and she carried a microphone in her hand. A cameraman stepped out behind her.

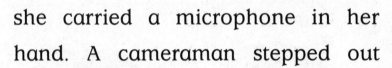

"It's Abby Anchor, the news reporter!" Melanie exclaimed. "And she's coming this way!"

Everyone looked to see what would happen next.

The reporter walked up to the crowd and said, "Excuse me, I'm looking for someone named Heidi Heckelbeck."

Heidi's mouth dropped open. "That's me!" she said. "But how do you know my name?"

The reporter looked over her shoulder. "These are my parents," she said. The elderly couple from the park stepped forward. "They told me about what you've done for Trace Park. Would you allow me to interview you?"

Heidi looked over to her parents for approval. "May I?" she begged. "May I *please* be on TV?"

Mom and Dad gave Heidi two thumbs-up.

"Hey, wait, what about me?" Henry asked. "Can I be on TV too? I picked up lots of trash with my robotic arm claw!"

The reporter stooped down. "I'd like to do a special segment on just *you*," she said.

Henry gasped and covered his mouth. Then he exclaimed, "Whoa! I'm going to be famous!"

Everyone laughed— even Heidi. Then the camera guy lifted the camera onto his shoulder and followed Heidi and Abby around the park.

The crowd watched and waved at the camera as Heidi showed off the work they'd done.

"These were made by our school principal and art teacher," Heidi said, pointing to the freshly stained park benches. "They also built three new picnic tables, and my friends helped stain them."

Bruce, Lucy, and Melanie waved at the camera.

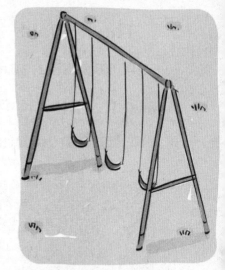

Heidi took Abby to the playground next.

"This swing set was donated by the Lancasters," Heidi explained. "And over here we have new teeter-totters donated by the Bickersons."

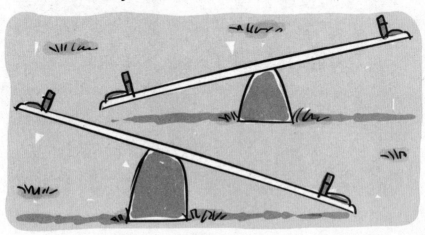

Then Heidi showed Abby the gardens she and Lucy had planted, along with the mowed meadows and the trimmed bushes and trees.

After Abby interviewed Henry, she asked all the volunteers to gather together. Heidi stood in front.

"You've done a great job, Heidi," Abby said live on camera. "Our whole community thanks you."

Everyone clapped.

"Looks like you're a real superstar," Aunt Trudy whispered, hugging her niece close.

"I couldn't have done it without you," Heidi whispered back.

Heidi could not believe it. The crowd, filled with her friends and family, cheered again.

Wow, Heidi thought. *Helping out was even more fun than casting a spell.*

Well, *almost.*

Check out the next book starring

HEiDi HECKELBECK

Heidi Heckelbeck handed a brown paper bag to her little brother. She had written his name, Henry Heckelbeck, on it.

"You can put YOUR thing-a-ma-bobs in here," she said. "And I'll put MY thing-a-ma-bobs in this bag."

Henry wrinkled his brow. "Okay.

But I have one question. What's a THINK-a-ma-bob?"

Heidi sighed loudly. "The word is 'THING-A-MA-BOB.' They are like doohickeys and random stuff we may need for this week. Do you understand?"

"Kind of," said Henry.

Heidi looked at the clock. "Ready? On your mark. Get set. GO!"

Then Heidi and Henry took off.

Henry ran to the desk in the kitchen and yanked open the top drawer. He stuck two rubber bands and a plastic spider in his bag.

Heidi found the leftover party

favor drawer and pulled out a purple tiara. There were also silver-and-pink beaded necklaces. Then she searched all the cupboards in the family room.

"Score!" she cried, holding up a can of unopened, neon-green Silly String. She plopped it into her bag.

Her next stop was the art supply cabinet. Heidi grabbed a tube of sequins, a handful of pom-poms, and a fistful of pipe cleaners. She had no clue how she was going to use all this stuff, but she would worry about that later.

An excerpt from *Heidi Heckelbeck and the Wacky Tacky Spirit Week*